CLYDE the HiPPO

CLYDE LIKES TO SLIDE

by Keith Marantz

illustrated by Larissa Marantz

PENGUIN WORKSHOP

PENGUIN WORKSHOP

An Imprint of Penguin Random House LLC, New York

Text copyright © 2020 by Keith Marantz. Illustrations copyright © 2020 by Larissa Marantz. All rights reserved. Published by Penguin Workshop, an imprint of Penguin Random House LLC, New York. PENGUIN and PENGUIN WORKSHOP are trademarks of Penguin Books Ltd, and the W colophon is a registered trademark of Penguin Random House LLC. Manufactured in China.

Visit us online at www.penguinrandomhouse.com.

Library of Congress Cataloging-in-Publication Data is available upon request.

ISBN 9780593094488 (paperback)   10 9 8 7 6 5 4 3 2 1
ISBN 9780593094495 (hardcover)   10 9 8 7 6 5 4 3 2 1

To Sasha, who wanted a puppy but couldn't have one because we already had a hippo in the backyard. To Kela, whose drawings started it all. And to Alek, who made us parents.

—KM & LM

This is Clyde.

Clyde likes to slide.

This is his first time on a slide at the park.

It is definitely NOT like the small one in his backyard.

Clyde isn't sure if he is ready for this.
Neither is his stuffed friend, Orson.

It seems a little too high up. Orson agrees.

goggles

helmet

parachute pack

umpire's vest

oven mitts

bubble wrap

knee pads

Clyde wishes he had prepared for this.

He shuts his eyes tight and imagines what could happen.

What if the slide is too hot?

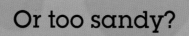

Or too sandy?

What if he goes down so fast,
he blasts into space like a rocket
and ends up on another planet?

What if he goes down so slowly,
it's dark when he reaches the bottom,
and everyone has gone home?

What if he goes down at just the right speed and gets stuck in the middle forever?

Or what if it starts to rain?

Clyde opens his eyes and decides he doesn't want to go down the slide, after all.

He turns around and sees his friend Toby, also awaiting possible doom.

"I don't want to go down!" Clyde says. "What if . . . ? What if . . . ?"

"What if *what*?" Toby asks.

Clyde takes a deep breath.

What if there is a good chance none of those things will happen?

He gulps, closes his eyes even tighter, and lets go.

When he reaches the bottom, he opens his eyes and sees his mother standing there, waiting for him.

"Are you okay, Clyde?" she asks.

"AGAIN! I want to do it again," Clyde exclaims.

"And this time, I'm going to keep my eyes OPEN!"

Clyde likes to slide!